Welcome to the NEW PARK!

TOYS

NEW!

For Ben, my FPV of boyhood!

And in memory of my sweet, scruffy Charlie-boy

• Little, Brown and Company • Hachette Book Group • 1290 Avenue of the Americas, New York, NY 10104 • Visit us at LBYR.com • First Edition: September 2019 • Little, Brown and Company is a division of Hachette Book Group, Inc. • The Little, Brown name and logo are trademarks of Hachette Book Group, Inc. • The publisher is not responsible for websites (or their content) that are not owned by the publisher. • Library of Congress Cataloging-in-Publication Data • Names: McCloskey, Shanda, author, illustrator. • Title: T-Bone the drone / Shanda McCloskey. • Description: First edition. | New York ; Boston : Little, Brown and Company, 2019. | Summary: Lucas is too busy with his new drone to play Wiffle ball with his friends, but when their only ball is captured by a mean dog, they retrieve it using teamwork and the drone. • Identifiers: LCCN 2018022810| ISBN 9780316510387 (hardcover) | ISBN 9780316510394 (ebook) | ISBN 9780316510356 (library edition ebook) • Subjects: | CYAC: Drone aircraft—Fiction. | Cooperativeness—Fiction. • Classification: LCC PZ7.1.M42215 Taaf 2019 | DDC [E]—dc23 • LC record available at https://lccn.loc.gov/2018022810 • ISBNs: 978-0-316-51038-7 (hardcover), 978-0-316-51039-4 (ebook), 978-0-316-51034-9 (ebook), 978-0-316-51036-3 (ebook) • PRINTED IN CHINA • 1010 • 10 9 8 7 6 5 4 3 2 1

ABOUT THIS BOOK: The illustrations for this book were done in watercolor, colored pencil, and Photoshop. This book was edited by Andrea Spooner and designed by Véronique Lefèvre Sweet. The production was supervised by Virginia Lawther, and the production editor was Marisa Finkelstein. The text was set in Imperfect and Zemke Hand ITC, and the display type is Slipstream and hand-lettered by the author.

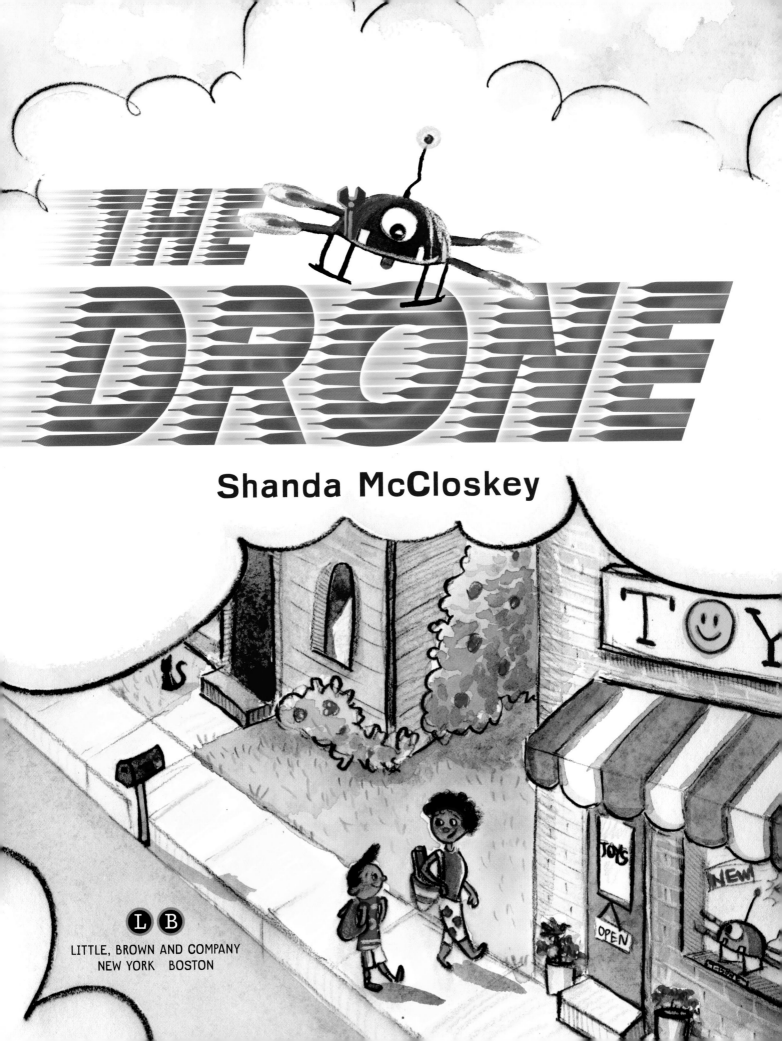

THE DRONE

Shanda McCloskey

L **B**

LITTLE, BROWN AND COMPANY
NEW YORK   BOSTON

When Lucas met T-Bone,
they were instant friends.

TOYS
on main street

OPEN

They learned together.

They ate together.

You like wrenches, huh?

They recharged together.

And Lucas had sweet dreams of flying together.

Still, Lucas was determined to get T-Bone *soaring*.

Lucas zoomed to the field to find his friends. Well, he *hoped* they were still his friends.

Yeah.
Go play
with your
space-dog.

Lucas stomped off the field
with T-Bone close by in
FOLLOW-ME mode.

Who needs
them anyway?
Let's fly, T-Bone!

T-Bone was wobbly at first, but soon he could glide and tilt and flip with ease. Then it happened.

A gust of wind, a dizzy drone, a swing, a hit, and...TINK!

If he was ever going to win his friends back, Lucas *had* to get that ball.

Lucas could hear low growls coming from some *THING* on the other side of the fence.

Lucas jolted upright.

The kids dumped out their bags
and emptied their pockets
to see what they had.

Candy canes?

Hooks!

These could come in handy! Get it?

Then they hatched a plan...

and built it!

It was finally time to put T-Bone to the test. Propellers hummed while Lucas maneuvered the drone up and over. *Bzzzzzzzzzzzz.*

Poor T-Bone came back pretty banged up, and the team was losing hope.

If Lucas could just see what was happening on the other side of that fence, maybe...

Lucas could "fly" *with* T-Bone.

With his goggles on, Lucas felt like he was floating as T-Bone *bzzzzzzed* over the fence.

"Ahhhhh! It looks vicious!"

When Lucas took off his goggles, he had never been prouder.

The kids were a team again—including T-Bone, their new ball retriever *and* mascot!

So...
how big was that
monster anyway?